WHAT VIENNA SAW

WHAT VIENNA SAW

Lyle Greenfield

are you sitting LLC

ISBN 978-1-09834-030-8

Published in the United States of America by Are You Sitting LLC, New York
PO Box 440 Amagansett, NY 11930

Cover and book design: Joan Greenfield / Gooddesign Resource
www.gooddesign.net

Please address all inquiries to: author@bangworld.com

For those who have seen in themselves
something not visible to the world.

"The most exciting attractions are between two opposites that never meet."

—Andy Warhol

WHAT VIENNA SAW

It's safe to say there was no residence in New York's far West Village in 1982 quite like Jordan Eklund's. In SoHo, of course, artists had been converting warehouse and factory lofts into studios and living spaces for years. Enormous, trashy-cool places to live and work and be a part of a still vibrant artistic community. But in 1982, the blocks close to the Hudson River, and the Meatpacking District were still Manhattan's 'wild west.' The idiosyncratic all-night bistro Florent didn't even exist then—the place was still a diner called the M&L, serving truck drivers and meatpacking workers in blood-stained butcher frocks in the daylight hours. The Belgian block streets were sticky with oil from the trucks and forklifts.

Jordan Eklund's residence occupied just over one-half of the 8th floor at 600 Washington Street. The one hundred ten-year-old factory building, which spanned the entire block between Horatio and Gansevoort streets, had been converted to warehouse lofts in the 70s, and he'd purchased the entire thing in 1979 for $985,000 cash, leaving the rental tenants where they were, till the leases expired. No rush. A cardboard warehouse, an office furniture warehouse, a restaurant supply place. The 8th floor, however, had been vacant for 7 years, since the previous tenant, Garnet Printing Company, had closed down and moved out, leaving two one-ton presses behind.

In the five years since Jordan Eklund had moved to the United States from Austria, he'd earned a small fortune in the art world serving, among other endeavors, as an associate curator at the Guggenheim, an advisor-buyer to several private client collectors, a forgery consultant to Sotheby's, as well as a collector of modern works himself. He even consulted for the NYPD and FBI in matters of art theft and forgery, identifying potential buyers of stolen works worldwide. Three years earlier Eklund had advised a discreet buyer from Tokyo, a friend of his father's, but the matter did not involve illegal property.

The Horatio St. entrance to the building looked blandly inhospitable, with its worn, faded marble floors, walls the color of coffee stains, battered metal elevator doors painted grey many times over, a heavy brass door leading to the stairwell. The elevator transported both people and freight. Only Jordan Eklund possessed the key to the 8th floor. A first-time visitor might gasp as the door slid open to the improbable sight of a vast open space of polished wooden floors, 14 ft. ceilings, white walls, giant double-hung windows facing the Hudson River to the west and partial views of the harbor and ferry boats to the south. In the center of this austere space a Bauhaus sofa and chairs surrounded a low, 8 ft. cast iron coffee table, overhung with an antique crystal chandelier. Ninety feet from the elevator an open kitchen and bar faced the room. To the right of that, an enormous workbench of thick, pitted wood served as a dining table. Behind the bench, a door leading to a large bath with floor and walls of ancient herringbone tile, a massive pedestal sink, and chipped claw foot tub. Next to the bath was the door to Jordan's bedroom, closed. And to the right hung a ten by ten-foot mirror framed in decorative cast iron.

Positioned here and there about the floor in a seemingly random yet precisely calculated display, sculptures by Inge King, Naum Gabo, Jacques Lipchitz, and Ben Nichelson silently demanded attention. A single Calder dangled above a lone wingback chair and cigar stand. Between the windows hung works by Robert Motherwell, Agnes Martin, Jean-Michel Basquiat, Bridget Riley, Warhol and others as yet unknown to the public.

At the age of 29, Jordan Eklund seemed an unlikely figure to command the respect and reputation he enjoyed. Physically, he appeared much younger, with his chiseled yet soft features, pale flesh, his thick, groomed dark blonde hair. Yet his tailored suits, Brioni or Huntsman, the bespoke shirts and ties, they made a certain statement. He wore them exclusively, whether in meetings or informal social gatherings in his gallery-loft. He never raised his voice but his facility with the language, in an unplaceable English-Austrian accent, demanded the listener lean forward and not interrupt. His demeanor was warm and welcoming, but not gregarious. Women found Jordan beautiful. Men did as well. All were confused by him, and mesmerized. In the end, that was a large part of the authority he possessed.

Late on the evening of Thursday, October 28, Jordan was gently ushering his guests out the door of his loft. The social 'meeting', which had included dinner (Chinese takeout) and drinks, had been attended by Jean-Michel Basquiat and his girlfriend Abrielle, gallerist Annina Nosei and representatives from her gallery, a publicist, and a somewhat detached John Perreault, art critic for the *Village Voice*. The purpose of the meeting involved the planning and publicizing of a brief showing of Basquiat's paintings at Annina Nosei Gallery, prior to their shipment to Fruitmarket Gallery in Edinburgh, Scotland for a major exhibition. Two of the works in that show were being loaned by Jordan—they would also travel the following week to Edinburgh.

As they waited for the elevator Annina turned to her host. "Thank you so much for putting up with us this evening, Jordan. I think it's going to be a fabulous show."

"I'm really quite excited about it, Annina. The exposure you've given Jean-Michel's work has been perfect—what a wonderful next step."

To which Basquiat replied, "Exposure? I've got a Krylon crew ready to spray a masterpiece on the side of your building, Jordan—say the word, my friend!" Which brought a chorus of laughter from the group.

"Perhaps when you return from Edinburgh we can discuss, Jean—you don't want to be distracted from the business at hand, now do you?"

The elevator arrived at the 8th floor with a chunking halt, the door opened, the guests exchanged handshakes, hugs, kisses and said their goodnights. When he heard the car reach the lobby floor, Jordan locked the door to 8. He brought plates and glasses to the kitchen sink and disposed of the takeout boxes and bags. Karina would clean up in the morning. He then walked over to the large mirror, staring at himself for a moment, removed his shoes then reached behind the raised iron frame for a recessed button, pressing it with his middle finger. With his right hand, he pushed the mirror easily three feet to the right, opened a heavy wooden door and walked forward into a dimly lit space. The door and mirror closed again behind him.

Jordan lifted a light switch on his left, illuminating three chandeliers hanging at 12-foot intervals through the center of a large room whose walls were covered in floral maroon velvet wallpaper bordered by gold-leafed crown and chair-rail moldings and hung with gold-framed mirrors and portraits of presumably 'royal' persons from a bygone era, as well as photographs of contemporary artists—Picasso, Warhol, Pollock, Haring—and of Josephine Baker. The room was furnished and arranged as a near replica of Tsaritsa Alexandra's sitting room in the Winter Palace in St. Petersburg.

Jordan heard the phone ring in the room he had left behind. He would let a message be left and perhaps return the call in the morning, continuing past a plush canopy bed draped with silk tapestries and into an intimate alcove. Jordan stood in front of a Victorian dressing table, divided in the middle by a full-length mirror, and removed all of his clothing, folding each item—jacket, shirt, pants—and placing them on a nearby settee. He watched himself in the mirror, his slender nearly hairless white body, his straight shoulders, narrow, childlike torso and hips. The long arms and fingers, and delicate neck.

He sat before the mirror on a velvet dressing stool and opened one of the table drawers, removing two small silicone breasts, which he sprayed lightly with an adhesive mist and placed carefully over his own pale breasts. At once they seemed a natural part of his body. From the same drawer, she removed a black silk lace brassiere, placing it over her breasts and fastening it in back. On the dressing table top was a soapstone bust of Lillian Gish, and upon her head a raven black wig with short, feathered bangs, shoulder length on the sides and back and a small bun woven on top, made from the hair of a young Chinese girl. She removed the wig from Miss Gish's head and carefully fitted and pinned it onto her own. Already her beauty could gaze back at her and she paused to reflect. Then, from a palette of makeup choices, she began applying a light cake to her face, above and below her eyes, emphasizing her porcelain skin. Next, she brushed the slightest albinos pêche dust onto her cheeks, painted the thinnest possible black line along her eyelids, carefully brushed her lashes and eyebrows a midnight rouge. Finally, she delicately brushed her lips with a dark, scarlet gloss, taking care to stay within the lip line.

Opening a walnut jewelry box, she stirred the glittering contents, picking out a blue tanzanite necklace and earrings, a gold band bracelet and sculptured silver rings for each finger of her right hand.

She stood before the mirror and whispered something to herself, then removed from another drawer a sheer, black brief and stockings, pulling them over her legs, buttocks and genitalia effortlessly. Against the wall to her left stood a large, open armoire. Without hesitation she chose a vintage three-quarter length black satin sheath with a high neckline and long sleeves, a short-waisted, midnight blue jacket, blue Victorian ankle booties, and dressed. The open doors of the armoire were mirrored, and she approved of herself from all angles. Turning back to the dressing table again she pulled a black Coq plume from a pin cushion and pushed the quill into her hair. In the mirror, a faint smile glanced approval. She grabbed a black, beaded clutch, left the dressing alcove and walked across the great room to a large, framed mural-like painting of Furore, on the Amalfi Coast. To the left, from a row of iron Mission hooks, she chose a cerulean blue silk scarf, throwing it around her neck and shoulders, then pushed the painting to the right, revealing the open door of an enormous freight elevator on the Horatio Street side of the building. She walked in, moved the painting, whose backside was simply unfinished plywood with the word C L O S E D stenciled on it, to its former position obscuring the elevator. She pressed 1 for the ground floor freight entrance and loading dock.

It was after midnight when she left the building, the heavy steel door locking behind her. Clutching her scarf close to her neck against the late October chill, she walked down the concrete steps and across Gansevoort to a waiting car. The driver got out, wearing a grey tweed jacket and Scottish tam, and opened the rear door.

"Good evening, Miss Martel."

"Good evening, Thomas, nice to see you on this chilly night," she replied in a voice approximately one semitone higher in pitch than Jordan's, with a faint French inflection and timbre far softer, more sensual.

"Yes, ma'am, not too warm, but the heater's on." Vienna Martel stepped into the back seat. "Will you be going to Ruby's tonight?"

"Yes, Ruby's." Thomas closed the door, returned to the driver's seat and circled the one-way blocks back onto Washington Street then, eight blocks later, right on Charles Street, right again on West Street and finally right onto tiny Charles Lane. Halfway into the block a dozen people were milling about, smoking cigarettes and joints near a short velvet rope leading to an unmarked red door three steps below the sidewalk.

Ruby's was a very different experience from what were considered the 'rough' gay bars and clubs just a short distance away. Places like The Mine Shaft and The Anvil, where patrons from all over the city would gather, seeking hard-core adventure among a simpatico tribe. Ruby's offered something far less carnal—a sensual fantasy set to music in a sophisticated parlor lounge. Thomas pulled up slowly near the curb, got out and opened the door for his passenger. "Miss Martel."

"Thank you, Thomas—I shouldn't be more than 2 hours."

"Yes, ma'am. I'll be right here." With that, she turned toward the small crowd and the red door, as several familiar faces greeted her. "Hi, Vienna!" "Hello, beautiful!" To which she replied warmly, "Hello, Alex…Hi, Manny." Music could be heard coming from inside. Duran Duran, fomenting the mood. *"Mouth is alive with juices like wine…and I'm hungry like the wolf…"* A tall black doorman in suit and tie welcomed her and opened the door.

"Hello, Miss Vienna. Have a wonderful night."

"Thank you, Jerome—I'll be sure to." And into the dark space she walked, the music much louder, past a narrow vestibule and cloakroom, into an intimate lounge area with patrons, many in Venetian or Mardi Gras masks, crowded near a mahogany bar on the right and in plush banquettes and ottomans to the left. Beyond the bar, a low archway led to a packed dance floor surrounded by low candlelit tables and chairs against brick walls hung with sconces and black and white photographs of Downtown street people. A small stage at the back of the room sometimes hosted unannounced performances from early New Wave legends and a weekly drag fashion show. This night a DJ was playing dance hits and 70's funk for the pre-Halloween celebrants jumping wildly and singing along to Culture Club and Human League. *"DON'T YOU WANT ME BABY? DON'T YOU WANT ME OOOH?"*

Vienna didn't pass through the archway. Instead, she was greeted by Ruby himself, a short, round man wearing a blue satin jacket, black shirt and ascot who spoke in a high, theatrical voice.

"Welcome, Vienna!" he nearly shouted, touching her shoulder and kissing both cheeks. "So good to see you always! Your usual place?"

"That would be lovely, Ruby. Everyone looks so festive," she said as he led her to an elevated banquette facing the bar.

"Well it is Thursday night…oops, Friday morning! And Halloween is coming. Actually, it's already *here!* Can I bring you something with bubbles?"

"You know me well." Ruby bowed and turned back to the bar. Vienna was more than a 'regular' at Ruby's. Since shortly after its opening in '80 she'd come three, even four times a week. Jordan had heard about the place from one of Jean-Michel's friends, but Jordan Eklund seldom went out late at night. Vienna had thought it sounded interesting, and so it turned out to be. She knew and was friendly with many of the patrons, and of course the bartender and staff, but never intimate with any. Pleasantries and small talk. When asked about herself she pulled from a menu of responses. "Everything's wonderful, and you?" "Yes, it's unbearably cold!" "I'm meeting a friend from Rome for lunch." "No, I'm much too tired to dance." Her beauty and reserve conveyed a certain mystery in an otherwise uninhibited spot and with it, an unspoken deference.

She recognized many faces of course, but others were hidden

behind their masks. Near the end of the bar, she noticed an older Japanese gentleman in a light grey suit, holding a soft leather bag. He had a thin, white mustache. He appeared to be alone, glancing toward the entrance frequently, sipping a short, brown drink. She knew him. Actually, Jordan knew him. Moments later Ruby returned with a glass of Champagne. "Voila!"

"Merci, Ruby." Vienna took the stem and raised it to her host, then her lips.

"De rien, Vienna—enjoy!" And with that Ruby pirouetted and returned to the front of the house.

Vienna took a sip from her glass, then noticed that the Japanese man was now speaking with two men wearing feathered mardi gras masks. One wore a long leather coat, the other a sport jacket over a red tee shirt. There seemed to be some disagreement among them. The old man shook his head and waved off whatever had been said with his finger. The man in the long coat held up both hands, palms facing out, as if insisting. The old man continued to shake his head. With his right hand obscured by the bar, the masked man removed a gun with a long barrel from his pocket and fired the gun at the old man's chest three times. He stood, frozen in shock for an instant, and reached for the mask facing him as his assailant pulled the bag from his hand. Vienna saw the gunman's face and their eyes met…she thought she recognized him, but from where? He dropped the bag, quickly put the mask back in place and the gun in his pocket. She saw the old man buckling. Nothing could be heard above the music and the crowd. She stood and stared as the accomplice held the old man up. The shooter picked up the bag, grabbed his partner by the shoulder, shouted something in his ear and he let the body fall to the floor and they left the club, bag in hand, as Vienna ran toward the bar, shouting Ruby's name.

The bartender, seeing Vienna, quickly moved toward her, assuming she'd wanted something, but now she was on the floor, loosening the old man's collar. She looked up, anguished, and spoke firmly, "A man's been shot, Tony, call the police!" Kneeling beside the body, Vienna opened his blood-soaked suit jacket, his white shirt glistening crimson. Ruby made his way to Vienna and gasped.

"Oh my god, Oh my god! Get back, get back everyone," as he pushed people away from where the body lay.

"We need water and towels…and an ambulance," Vienna demanded. "He's been shot—two men did it, and now they've gone."

"Yes, of course! Of course!" Ruby shouted instructions to the bartender who was already on the house phone.

"Police are on the way! An ambulance, too," Tony announced as he hung up the phone.

On the dance floor, the crowd was oblivious to what had happened. The DJ had his headphones on, "Tainted Love" filled the room. Ruby felt it best to contain the crisis to the bar area, till police came. Out on the sidewalk, no one knew what had happened. The two men had left the club, calmly if briskly, entered a waiting car and driven off. Within 5 minutes sirens screamed and two police cars pulled up abruptly, effectively blocking Charles Lane. Three cops rushed out and into the club. One stayed outside, instructing the now curious onlookers to stay where they were, and away from the door. Thomas got out of the limousine and rushed over to the cop.

"Officer, can you tell me what's going on?"

"Someone's been shot—stay clear of the entrance, an ambulance is on the way."

"My passenger is inside, sir, and she's alone—I have to see that she's all right." With that Thomas bolted toward the door but was grabbed at the elbow by Officer White, a large, muscular black man.

"Sir, no one's going inside at this point. You'll wait outside till the crime scene is cleared. Now back away."

Charging inside to the bar area the cops wedged into the crowd and quickly saw the body on the floor, Ruby and the bartender crouched, and Vienna kneeling, applying clean towels to the gushing wounds. Officer Molina spoke first. "Please stand back everyone. Stand back! What happened here?"

Ruby, gasping for breath, answered. "This man was shot. I don't know if he's alive." One of the cops, Officer Huang, knelt by the body and tried to find a pulse at his neck.

"He has no pulse," she informed routinely.

"Are you the owner here?" Officer Molina asked.

"Yes."

"No one is allowed to leave the premises—tell your people now." Ruby instructed Tony to inform the staff.

"Did anyone see the shooting?"

Ruby looked down at Vienna. "She may have seen it—Vienna was the first to alert us."

Vienna shot a frozen glance at her friend and stood.

"Ma'am, did you see what happened here?"

"Yes. I saw the shooter."

"Could you give me a little more detail please?" Molina drilled, a bit impatiently.

"He fired his gun three times. There were two men—first, they were all talking, then they grabbed a leather bag from him, shot him and left the club."

"Could you identify the two men?"

Vienna hesitated, considering her answer. There was much to consider. "Perhaps one of them. They were both wearing masks."

"Like ski masks?"

"No. Like mardi gras masks."

"If they were wearing masks, how could you identify them, or one?"

"When he fired his gun the old man reached for his mask and pulled it down before collapsing."

"Were you standing here, close by?"

"I was sitting there," she pointed to the banquette against the wall."

"Did anyone else see what happened?"

"I don't know. It was crowded and the music loud."

"And how did you...happen to notice what was happening?"

Vienna paused but held her gaze on the officer. "I thought it odd, seeing the older Japanese man here, wearing a suit, holding his bag—I was, I guess you could say, studying him."

"Do you know this man?" Officer Molina asked, indicating the body at his feet.

"No, I do not."

A siren could be heard outside as an ambulance step van from New York Presbyterian arrived. A nurse and EMT got out, pulled a gurney from the rear and headed into the club. Those standing near the bar were herded into the banquette area. The music stopped and the third cop, Officer Riley, shouted instructions that no one was to leave the club. There's been a shooting. The situation is under control. You will be free to go shortly…please stand or sit quietly.

The gurney was beside the body now as the nurse knelt to find a pulse. There was none. He quickly opened the man's shirt and applied defibrillator suctions to his chest, near the bullet holes, and started the device. The torso shook, but after a full 50 seconds there was no heartbeat, no breathing. The nurse looked up. "He's gone, I'm afraid. We'll take him to Presbyterian." The body was lifted onto the gurney, strapped in and rolled toward the door. Officer Molina interrupted before they could exit.

"Wait, please. Does he have a wallet?" He didn't wait for an answer, reaching inside the suit jacket and pulling out a leather billfold, rifling through it. Several hundred in cash, credit cards, driver's license. He read the name out loud. "Yusaku Saji, 985 Fifth Avenue. "Yusaku Saji," he repeated under his breath. Vienna recognized the name but remained silent.

"Officer, we need to take the wallet with us—you can claim it in an hour, once the body's been checked into the morgue. We copy all the documents." Officer Molina handed the wallet to the nurse, the gurney proceeded to the sidewalk.

"Officer, I need to let my customers go home and clean this up!" Ruby pleaded, but the cop was unmoved.

"Sir, this is a crime scene. The crime was murder. Everyone will leave but only when we see the ID and have the names and contact information of each person in the premises, including the staff and yourself. Officer Riley, Huang, please inform everyone here—names, addresses, ID. Then they can leave." Turning to Vienna, who stood beside Ruby, he spoke evenly, "Miss, it appears you may have been the only witness to this. I'll need you to come to the station with me and give a statement. Sorry for the inconvenience." A great sense of alarm flashed through Vienna's mind and body, though not betrayed on her face.

"I've told you everything that I saw," she protested, "everything I know, and I know nothing further."

"It's just procedure ma'am. You're not a suspect, but we'll need your statement. It'll be another half hour here at most."

"My driver is waiting outside."

"Then he can follow us, understood?" Vienna returned to the banquette where she'd been sitting just 22 minutes earlier. A million thoughts rushed through her head. Jordan had meetings, starting in mid-morning. He would need at least a few hours' sleep.

The cops processed the exiting partiers with surprising efficiency—they had no interest in hanging around Ruby's either. Masks off, check ID, make note of names, addresses, phone. A couple underage boys, who would simply be warned. Photos had been taken of the body where it lay, and the room, the bar. There was no way to dust for prints—a hundred hands had been on that bar. The assailants weren't drinking. The only thing they'd gripped was the bag and the gun, both of which left the club with them. Frustrating. By 1:40 a.m. the place was nearly empty, except for the staff, and Vienna. Ruby was instructed to do nothing at the spot of the shooting, the perimeter of which had been taped off on the floor and bar. No cleaning, no moving stools. Detectives would return in the morning to fill in any missing details. He should be available to let them in—they would call first. Officer Molina looked over to Vienna. "Miss, please come with me—this shouldn't take long."

Vienna and Molina left the club with Officer Huang. Officers Riley and White would follow once the place was empty and locked and the street cleared of lingering patrons wanting to talk, speculate, argue about what had happened. Thomas approached Vienna as she was being ushered to the police vehicle. "Miss Martel…"

"It's all right, Thomas. I have to go with the police. Can you follow us and wait please?"

"Yes, ma'am, of course."

"Thank you." Officer Huang opened the back door of the police car and Vienna stepped inside. The light bar flashed, the siren screamed as Thomas ran back to the Mercedes and followed the speeding car to the West 10th Street station.

Inside, it may have been the 'graveyard shift' but in the relentless wash of fluorescent lighting, time stood still. Dispatcher on two phones, booking desks occupied, men in cuffs waiting to be 'processed,' metal partitions taped with photos of wives, kids, parents, the smell of thirty-year-old upholstery and day-old coffee. Officer Molina led Vienna to his cubicle and a chair by his desk. Pen in hand and a stained yellow legal pad at the ready, he began the tedious line of questioning. "Please state your full name."

"Vienna Juliette Martel."

"Could I see your ID?" Vienna pulled a thin wallet from her clutch and produced a drivers license, betraying none of the anxiety she felt churning inside her. "It's French," observed Molina as he examined the car.

"Yes."

"Is that where you're from? France?"

"Yes, Paris. I'm living here temporarily."

"What is it you do, Miss Martel?"

"I'm a writer."

"What is it you write?"

"Fiction and non-fiction. It depends. Is this what you wanted to speak with me about, Officer?" Molina massaged his forehead and returned to mundane protocol.

"Your address in New York…"

"600 Washington Street. The entrance is on Gansevoort."

"Is there an apartment number?"

"The 8th floor. Number 801."

"Your phone number please."

"2-1-2…3-4-2-6-8-1-6"

"Tell me what you saw tonight at the club. Every detail, please, from the moment you entered." Vienna repeated everything she had already reported to the officer as they'd stood beside the body. There was no inconsistency though perhaps more detail: what the assailants wore, the long barrel of the gun, presumably a silencer, how long the encounter lasted, what she did when she saw the shooting… "And you said that you saw the shooter's face…"

"Briefly, when his mask was pulled down."

"Do you think you would recognize him if you saw him again?" She paused, trying to imagine the consequences of her answer.

"I believe so."

"And did he see you?" She reflected on this for a moment. "Did the killer see you, Miss Martel?" Officer Molina repeated.

"Yes. I think so." Molina paused, then looked up.

"How old do you think he was? His race? The basics please."

"Perhaps in his mid-thirties. White, maybe 185 centimeters. Angular features, thick, medium length hair…" Molina interrupted, while still writing.

"And you said you didn't recognize the victim, um, Yusaku Saji?"

"I did not."

"All right, this is good, Miss Martel. We'll need you to return later today and sit with a sketch artist and give this description again, in as much detail as possible."

"No. I have business during the day. I'm sorry but I can't come back here."

"Then he can meet you at your home if you prefer." Her thoughts raced from her mind to her stomach with sickening speed.

"No. I could come in the late afternoon."

"Could we say 4p.m.? I'll make the arrangements."

"Yes. May I leave here now?" It was just after 2:50 on Friday morning.

"Of course. I'll walk you to the door, make sure your ride is still waiting." Her car was parked directly in front and Thomas stepped out immediately upon seeing his client.

"Thank you for your time, Miss Martel. We'll see you tomorrow—I mean later today." Vienna nodded "Yes," not looking back as she hurried to the car. Thomas opened the door.

"Thank you, Thomas."

"Home now, Miss Martel?"

"Please." No words were spoken on the short ride to Gansevoort. Vienna manipulated the puzzle over and over again in her mind. How could she come to the police station… in daylight? Jordan had work to do, and meetings. Probably just a few calls to be made in the morning. The car pulled up to the dimly lit curbside and Thomas got out to open the door for Vienna.

"Can I walk you to your door, Miss Martel?"

"Thank you, Thomas, that won't be necessary."

"I'm sorry about this terrible thing tonight, I wish…"

"The police will sort it out, I'm sure. Would you be able to pick me up tomorrow, well this afternoon, at 3:50, Thomas? I have to go back there."

"Yes, ma'am, I can be here." She reached into her clutch and removed two one hundred dollar bills, pressing them into his hand.

"Thank you for staying tonight. Now get some rest and I'll see you this afternoon." Vienna turned and walked to the building, up the concrete steps and into the freight elevator.

It was Jordan who'd provided Thomas with an introduction to Vienna three years earlier. At the time, Thomas was driving a Checker Cab four nights a week. On one of those nights, he'd picked Jordan up on Washington Street and driven him to Brooklyn Heights, for a dinner party hosted by an East Side gallery owner. A twenty-minute ride across town and over the Brooklyn Bridge. Enough time to learn that the driver had left his "dead end" union job unloading shipping containers on the docks in Baltimore, that his younger brother had been shot and killed in the street after a bar fight, that he'd thought he should get his shit together and go back to school, was enrolled as a freshman, at the age of 31, at St. Francis College in Brooklyn, was studying psychology and criminal justice with the idea of maybe going to law school, was living with his sister in Queens, but just for now. Enough time for Jordan to sense that his driver was street-smart, and working to get something better than what he'd come from, enough time to tell him he knew of someone who was looking for a driver, usually at night, who could provide a car…and would he be interested in speaking with her? "Sure, I'd be willing to talk to her," he'd replied as the cab pulled in front of a brownstone on Clark Street. And the car that Vienna could provide was Jordan's 1960 Mercedes 300D, ownership of which he'd assigned to her after realizing it was simpler to walk or take cabs than bother with a car. But *she* shouldn't be walking *or* looking for a cab at 2 in the morning in the far West Village.

"Her name is Vienna Martel and she lives on Gansevoort Street. I'll let her know to expect your call. You can tell her Jordan gave you her number—if you have a piece of paper, I'll write it down for you." The driver handed Jordan his copy of *The Daily News* and a pen, indicating the white space above the masthead. Jordan filled in the space and handed the paper back along with a twenty dollar bill. "I'm sorry, I didn't get your name."

"Thomas. Thomas Finnegan."

"Nice talking with you, Mr. Finnegan. Good luck in school."

"Thanks. I'll definitely call your friend." With that, Jordan left the cab and Thomas drove back to Manhattan.

Inside her home, Vienna locked the elevator to the 8th floor and slid the mural over the door again. She walked directly to the dressing alcove and studied her troubled face in the mirror. She held the back of her hand to her lips, whispering, "I'm sorry. It will be fine. It will be all right…I promise." Still standing, Vienna removed the Coq plume from her hair, then the wig, placing it back upon the bust of Miss Gish. She undressed, carefully returning her dress, jacket and shoes to the armoire. Next, the jewelry. Then her brassiere, followed by her breasts, which he placed back into the dressing table drawer. Jordan wearily stared at himself. "Sleep," he whispered and finished. Undergarments would go in the bottom drawer of the armoire for now. Naked, he gathered up his clothing, closed the French doors to the alcove and left Vienna's home, returning to his own.

The '78 Plymouth pulled into the warehouse garage on Pacific Street in Jersey City just before 2 a.m. A one-story, cinder block building with a few filthy wire security windows and two steel garage doors that housed Teddy Misko's trucking business. Which consisted of a small fleet of step vans he rented out to mostly commercial plumbing and electrical suppliers. The driver was Teddy's nephew, Dimitri. His passengers were freelancers who'd worked for Teddy in the past. They watched as he thumbed through the stacks of bills emptied from the leather bag onto a steel desk. Ten stacks, a hundred thousand per. A million dollars. He handed one to the taller man in the long leather coat. "Why the fuck would you kill him in the club for Christ' sake? You were supposed to take him out to the street, to the car…now it's a murder. They have a body… fucking hell."

"He refused to go outside. He wanted the thing brought inside. We didn't have it, you know that. The place was loud and crowded. Made sense."

"So no one saw you?"

"No. Maybe one person, at a distance."

"But you were wearing masks."

The accomplice, Danny, broke in. "After he was shot, and he's falling, the guy pulled Mika's mask down. But he had it back on in a second."

"But someone *might* have seen you?"

"This one chick," Mika answered. Teddy stared at him, disgusted.

"That's called a witness."

"Look, you've got your 900 thousand *and* the property—

we'll take care of this."

"How the fuck are you going to 'take care of this'?"

"We'll find out who she is."

"You think the police are just giving out her name? Jesus."

"Danny will go back to the club tonight, when they reopen the place."

Danny shook his head. "No, no way, I'm not going back in the fucking club!"

"No one fucking saw you...you're just another party boy. People will be talking about the shooting. You'll be shocked and buy a few drinks and wonder if anyone saw what happened. Then we'll have a name. Easy. Just change your fucking clothes—it's Friday night." Danny shook his head but kept quiet, resigned to what he had to do next. Teddy was unmoved by Mika's scheme.

"Hey! We have other business to do, but it can't get done till this is fixed. Dimitri, leave the Plymouth here—maybe somebody saw it. Take the blue Galaxy behind the shop and drive this one where he needs to go, then go straight home." Turning a hard look to Danny he ordered, "Don't take a car to the club. Probably be cops on the block. Taxi, subway, whatever. Call me by Sunday night and tell me this is handled."

It was 2:45 when they pulled away from Teddy Misko's garage in the Galaxy. Dimitri took the Holland Tunnel back to Manhattan and dropped Mika at his place on the Lower East Side, then over the Brooklyn Bridge taking 278 and Ocean Parkway to Sheepshead Bay and the walkup he and Danny shared in a nondescript row house. There was no traffic and little spoken along the way, the three running through the night's events in their heads. Danny mumbled, "This is fucked up" to himself. No answer required. Mika counted out 25 thousand from his stack and handed it to Danny, who stopped mumbling and recounted it. Dimitri would get his from Uncle Teddy—but only when everything was "handled."

Jordan Eklund was awakened from a fitful sleep by the phone beside his bed, just after 8:30 a.m. He rolled over, cleared his throat and picked up the receiver. "Hello, this is Jordan."

"Mr. Eklund, this is Detective Ronson from the Major Case Squad, NYPD downtown." This was not a social call.

"How can I help you, detective?" Now sitting on the bed, naked, Jordan quickly summoned his senses.

"Are you aware of the theft of a Kandinsky painting from a private residence yesterday morning?"

Jordan sat rigidly. "I was not aware. Who was the painting stolen from?"

"The Kellerman home, in Oyster Bay Cove."

"My god, I know the Kellerman's and I know the work... so..."

"We believe this theft may be related to a murder that took place last night at a club on Charles Lane in the Village. It's called Ruby's."

Jordan had not assembled the pieces in his brain at this point. "I don't understand."

"The victim was a Japanese businessman named Yusaku Saji. He was also a collector of fine art. And he was seen handing a leather bag to a man who then shot him three times and left the club with the bag. There was one witness, who will meet with a police sketch person today. Do you know Mr. Saji, Mr. Eklund?"

"Yes, I negotiated two sales on his behalf several years ago. Both recorded transactions—I'm shocked to hear this. You believe he was involved in the Kandinsky theft?" Jordan asked incredulously.

"We're not certain, but we'd like to get on top of this before the FBI gets involved, which will probably be Monday morning."

"Of what assistance could I be, detective?" Jordan Eklund found the thought of any involvement in this case extremely disturbing. Yet his calm belied his fears. "Of course, I want to help in any way I can. Do you know how the break-in occurred?"

"Well that's another reason we're seeking your expertise, sir. The theft was not a break-in."

"I'm sorry?" Jordan replied, confused.

"It was not a break-in," the detective repeated. "The painting was to be loaned to the Guggenheim as part of a Kandinsky exhibit. It was scheduled to be picked up by the museum's transport service yesterday afternoon. Two men in white jackets arrived in a step van at the Kellerman home late yesterday morning, claiming to be from Harrison Transport and were shown into the house by Mrs. Kellerman. She said they'd displayed proper ID. They carefully wrapped and removed the painting and were gone within fifteen minutes, even leaving her a copy of the signed receipt. Approximately four hours later the real transport vehicle, and the actual Harrison art handlers, showed up. That's when we got the call."

"Good god. And you believe these two events are somehow connected, the theft and the murder?" Jordan had already made the connection. The man whose face had been exposed to Vienna eight hours earlier was a security guard at the Guggenheim whom he had seen, though never known, on several occasions. Detective Ronson's call had set in motion a hallucinogenic collision of places and images inside Jordan Eklund's mind. His left hand pressed against his chest, his eyes closed.

"Yes, we think the timing's too close to call it a coincidence. We'd like you to come downtown tomorrow morning, Mr. Eklund—I can show you the sketch of the suspect then and perhaps you can tell me more about the victim, Mr. Saji…who else he might be doing business with, that kind of thing. Can we say 9 a.m.?" Jordan was silent, thinking about the hours that lay before him, like narrow boards strung across a bottomless canyon. Vienna had to be protected. "Will 9 a.m. work for you, Mr. Eklund?" the detective repeated.

"Yes. Yes, I can be there at 9, detective."

"Oh, and one more thing, Mr. Eklund. It seems that the witness lives in your building, on Gansevoort Street."

"In *my* building?" Jordan asked, with a combination of real and amplified alarm. "What is his, or her, name?"

"Her name is Vienna Martel. She lives on the 8th floor. I presume you know her."

"Yes, of course I know her. She's rented the space from me since 1980, though I seldom encounter her as I live and work on the Horatio Street side. But that's very interesting indeed, detective." In truth, it was more than "interesting" to Jordan that the police had already placed Vienna in his building. It was unnerving.

"Well we can speak more about your tenant tomorrow, Mr. Eklund. It's 1 Police Plaza, Park Row."

"Yes, I know where you are. Till then." Jordan hung up the phone and stood. There wasn't time to review his 'options' at the moment, nor Vienna's for that matter. Karina would arrive at 10 to clean the loft. Annina's people would arrive at 11 to wrap and remove the two Basquiat's to her gallery before they departed for the Edinburgh show. Vienna needed time to prepare for her appointment at the 6th Precinct station. He would reschedule his luncheon meeting with one of Sotheby's 'client liaisons.' Jordan quickly made his bed, walked to the bath and stepped into a hot shower. A cleansing, a calming of the surface. If only the water could run over his brain, and his organs, comfort them like a fetus in the womb. After five minutes he shut off the hot water and rinsed with the cold. His senses jumped to attention, shutting down his reverie and focusing on the things to be done in the next six hours. Addressing the first of those, he stood in front of the old pedestal sink, leaned close to the mirror and shaved the barely visible fine hairs from his face. He dressed in a light grey wool and silk suit, white shirt, dark blue tie with muted maroon stripes. Business could begin.

Jordan pushed the enormous mirror to the side and entered
Vienna's home. He seldom saw the place in daylight and it was
a bit disarming—colder certainly in the indiscriminate light of
day than beneath the soft highlights of the chandeliers. He felt
almost as though he were invading her privacy. Entering the
dressing alcove he considered himself for a moment in front of
the mirror. He removed his clothing and once again sat on the
dressing stool and placed the small breasts over his own. Then
a blue silk brassiere and, again, the wig, which she positioned
on her head. Today, no coq plume. Today, a 'practical' face,
a matte pêche-rose lipstick. There weren't so many daytime
options in Vienna's wardrobe. She chose a simple cerise silk
blouse, pleated wool slacks, ankle boots, cerulean leather waist
jacket. A plain silver ring for the forefinger of her right hand.
Finally, a burnt umber and saffron silk scarf tied close to her
neck. It was autumn, after all. She picked up the beaded clutch
again and gave a faint smile to herself—quite stunning for a
late midday appearance.

Vienna left the alcove and lingered near the bed briefly. The
bed she had rarely lay upon. She lay across it now and, closing
her eyes, began to conjure the events of last night, rather,
early that morning, in Ruby's. The man's face. How she would
describe him to the police sketch person. Definitely not his
identity. That would be up to Jordan, once they showed him
the sketch. She sat up, stood up and left the daylit room,
locking the doors behind her. Outside, Thomas stood waiting
beside the Mercedes on Horatio Street.

"Hello, Miss Martel," he offered, opening the rear door.

"Hello, Thomas—thank you for being here."

"Yes, ma'am, always a pleasure." She stepped inside and he returned to the driver's seat. "You said the 6th Precinct station? I hope everything is all right."

"Yes, they want me to describe the man I saw to a sketch person—I'm sure it will be fine. Can you wait for me there?"

"Of course."

It was exactly 4:00 p.m. when Vienna walked into the station house on West 10th. The place looked exactly as it had 13 hours earlier except there were more cops milling around inside, more clerks at desks and more people waiting to be processed or listened to. She approached a receiving desk and announced herself to a sturdy female police officer, Officer McGrath. "Can I help you?" she asked blankly.

"I have a 4 o'clock appointment, arranged by Officer Molina."

"Your name."

"Vienna Martel."

"Officer Molina is gone for the day. You'll be meeting with Mr. Kwan. Please take a seat, I'll let him know you're here."

"I'll stand, thank you." Officer McGrath dialed the sketch artist's extension, spoke, hung up.

"He's coming out."

Mr. Heng Kwan was not in uniform because he was not a cop. A wiry, middle-aged man with straight grey hair and inquisitive brown eyes, he wore khaki pants, a flannel shirt, corduroy jacket and wire-rimmed glasses. He was friendly and approachable. "Miss Martel?"

"Yes."

"I'm Heng Kwan. Can you come with me, please?" He led Vienna out of the common area and down a hall to a small, windowless office on the right. Three vinyl upholstered steel chairs, one steel desk, metal file cabinets, one wooden drawing table and rolling stool, and on the walls, an assortment of faces in pencil from crimes gone by. He positioned one of the chairs beside the table and the stool behind it, where he would work.

"Please sit here, Miss Martel," Kwan said, holding the chair for her.

He then sat behind the table and picked up a pencil. "Before we begin, do you have any questions?"

Vienna, annoyed, answered quickly. "How long do you expect this to take, Mr. Kwan?"

"Well, that will depend upon how quickly we can closely render on paper the face you recall seeing, miss. It could be a half hour…it could be over an hour. Shall we begin?"

"Yes, please."

"Let's start with the most basic features first—he is male, is that correct?"

"Yes."

"Okay, his ethnicity, age, the shape of his head, neck, hair— then we can begin to fill in the features."

Vienna placed his age at 36. Caucasian. His head fairly large, not bulbous. Slightly chiseled, somewhat prominent jaw, perhaps Eastern European. Kwan sketched quickly, like the caricature artists in Central Park. As Vienna watched she corrected his lines: *raise the cheekbones a bit…his chin has a slight cleft...a prominent ridge above the eyebrows...* Erase. Sketch. Erase. Sketch. Erase... Even as the portrait drew closer to a likeness, she grew impatient with the process. Vienna rose from her chair and stood near the artist, leaning over his shoulder.

"Mr. Kwan, would you mind please, just for a moment?" she asked but actually instructed as she reached for his pencil and bent over the drawing table. Kwan was nonplussed, but pushed his stool backwards to make room for the interloper. Vienna erased the hairline, then lowered and thickened it slightly. Erased the tip of the nose, squaring it somewhat and bringing the nostrils closer to center. Softened the cheekbones, thinned the lips, deepened the nasolabial folds. In moments Vienna's alterations brought the portrait closer to a photographic representation of the man she had seen at Ruby's and whom Jordan now recognized as a security guard at the Guggenheim. She studied the rendering, feathered the sideburns partially over the ears, then stood, satisfied, handing the pencil back to Kwan. "Thank you. That's the man I saw." She began to turn away from the drawing board.

"But miss, we haven't quite, um, finished..." He felt an instinctive need to regain control of the session's outcome. But the session was over.

"That's the man I saw," Vienna repeated, "thank you, Mr. Kwan." She turned and left the office and the 6th Precinct station. Waiting idly beside the car, Thomas quickly focused when Vienna emerged onto the sidewalk.

"Everything all right, Miss Martel?" he asked while opening the passenger door.

"Yes, thank you, Thomas. A bit tedious is all."

"Is there anywhere else?"

"Just home, please. And I won't be going out this evening, but I will call you again tomorrow."

"Yes, ma'am." Thomas drove back to Gansevoort Street. There were no further words between driver and passenger as Vienna stared out the window and deep into her thoughts. Jordan would have calls to return. Dinner at Raoul's had been planned with Jean-Michel, Abrielle and Annina—an early celebration of the gallery show. Sleep would be important. If difficult to imagine.

It was already after 5 as Vienna reentered her home. Still daylit, she illuminated the chandeliers—a shimmering, familiar comfort. Sitting on her bedside she constructed the future. Then reconstructed. She could not be a 'witness' in a court of law. She could not make herself a public figure. Jordan would be asked to testify, for god's sake. She shook her head and walked into the dressing alcove. Staring into the mirror, her eyes moistened. She saw her very existence fluttering like a rippled reflection on the surface of a pond. She and Jordan had been born of the same womb, on the same day in 1954, at the University Hospital of Zurich. Yet he hadn't recognized her presence inside of him until he was ten, or eleven. An age when he was too young to understand his feelings, or what she was trying to tell him. Too ashamed to acknowledge his longings. But it was the art world his parents inhabited that had helped him see and feel what was possible, through the erotic images of Balthus, Picasso, Édouard-Henri Avril, and others—and through the lives of those strange creatures themselves. By age thirteen, Jordan and Vienna had begun to exist as equals, their minds and souls inseparable since their shared cognizance. She would never have chosen to leave him, but now the question of choice, of so-called "free will," had been narrowed. Perhaps shut down entirely. When we are told we have three months to live, or three weeks, or three days, do we think about living that time to the fullest? Preparing our soul for what might or might not be next? Making amends for…whatever? Or anesthetizing ourselves from the terrifying clarity at hand? Would Vienna ever see herself again? Would she ever *be* herself again? She touched her face softly with her hand.

And undressed herself. But this time Jordan would leave Vienna's home with her silk blouse, her pleated slacks, cerulean jacket, scarf, the ankle boots, the clutch. He also took her silicone breasts, brassiere, and Vienna's wig, all that she was last seen wearing, being, in public, uncertain she would ever return.

In his loft, Jordan was careful to remove all traces of Vienna's makeup. He fingered the slightest bit of pomade into his hair and brushed it into place. There were messages from the Curator of Contemporary Art at the Guggenheim (undoubtedly calling about the Kandinsky theft); Annina confirming dinner; Chiaki Saji, daughter of Yusaku Saji; an insurance adjuster; the cardboard warehouse tenant (a water leak). He would call Annina and Chiaki, deal with the water leak and wait till tomorrow for the rest. It was too much for now.

Over dinner at Raoul's the conversation could hardly be described as a 'celebration' of Jean-Michel's brilliant successes. Instead, the topics turned quickly to theft and murder.

"So, the woman actually *let* the thieves into her home and *watched them* wrap and remove the painting?" Basquiat asked mockingly.

"It appears that's exactly what happened," Jordan replied. "The actual transport handlers from the museum arrived hours later, as originally scheduled."

"That's fucking crazy," Abrielle dropped, incredulously.

"And police are imagining there may be some connection between the theft and the murder at Ruby's, Jordan?"

"They believe it shouldn't be ruled out, Annina, given that the victim was a well-known art collector, and a client of mine—it's a bit unnerving, but we shall see. But why don't we offer a toast to our dear friend, who happens to be very much alive at this table right now!"

At 10:15 p.m. Danny took the Q, then the 3 train from Sheepshead Bay to 14th Street in Manhattan. Just under an hour. He would walk the rest of the way to Ruby's on Charles Lane. Maybe 20 minutes, or a little more. A chilly, clear night—a chance to gather his thoughts before reentering the scene of the crime. His crime. Danny hated the idea. Wished he was having a beer and a shot back at the Towne Cafe right now. Fuck it—this was the deal. In his blue sateen shirt, sensible gold chain, black leather sport jacket and tight black jeans Danny looked like he might 'fit in' at Ruby's, even if he didn't feel he fit in. Fuck it.

It was nearly midnight when he arrived in front of the club, wound tightly but looking forward to a first drink. He saw a police car parked maybe 50 feet away, two cops inside. A few young men loitered on the sidewalk with their smokes. Jerome was once again at the door as Danny approached the short velvet rope. "That's 25 dollars, sir," he said, interrupting his forward motion.

"Oh, right," he replied, fishing for cash from his back pocket and handing over two 10s and a 5.

"I'll just stamp your hand," which he did quickly, leaving "Ruby's" in ruby red ink on the back of Danny's right hand. Jerome held the door and he proceeded inside the club, where he'd been less than 24 hours earlier.

He hated being there. Ruby stood, soberly, by the near end of the bar. There were only six others at the bar and just a few seated on the ottomans and banquettes to the left. Fewer still in the other room, and no one on the dance floor. The music mix was strangely disconnected, from Stan Getz's Bossa Nova to Donna Summer, Sinatra, Culture Club… The patrons spoke quietly. There was no revelry inside Ruby's on this night. Danny stood with both hands on the bar rail and Tony acknowledged immediately.

"What can I get you?"

"Stoli and tonic. Slice of lime." Seconds later the bartender pushed a tall glass in front of Danny.

"Do you want to start a tab?"

"No, I'll settle."

"That'll be nine dollars." Danny pulled out his wallet and handed Tony a ten. He was searching for words. They weren't coming easily.

"My friend told me about this place—said it was a great spot. But it seems kinda quiet for a Friday night…" Tony was uncertain how much to engage with this guy. Whom he didn't know.

"Well, there was an incident here last night, so it'll probably be quiet for a couple days. But Halloween will be another story."

"An incident?" Danny probed. A young man standing close by seized his opportunity to tell the tale.

"There was a shooting—a man was killed!" he blurted out as if privileged information.

"Jesus Christ, you're kidding!" Danny replied, feigning surprise.

"Not kidding!" Tony, eyeing Ruby, was not happy with this conversation. But Danny had found his opening.

"Did they get whoever did it?" he asked, feigning concern.

The young man's companion jumped in.

"He was wearing a mask and he walked out before anyone knew what happened. Gone!"

"Holy shit!" Danny exclaimed. "That's crazy!" Ruby moved closer to the three men, hoping to end the tiresome rehashing, which he found genuinely upsetting.

"My friends, it would be good if we didn't make last night's tragedy the topic of this evening's chit chat at Ruby's. You're welcome to do that outside, would that be all right?" he instructed.

"So nobody saw the guy who shot him?" Danny pursued.

"Vienna might have seen him, when his mask came off!" the young man's companion volunteered eagerly.

"Jason, respect Vienna's privacy for god's sake! This matter is in the hands of the police now."

"I'm sorry…this is just so…wild," Danny said apologetically. "Maybe I'll try to come back Halloween."

"It will be a proper party, I promise," Ruby said, walking back to his station at the front. Behind him, Danny continued out to the sidewalk again. He approached Jerome.

"Excuse me, have you seen Vienna tonight? I was supposed to meet her here."

"If you don't see Thomas, you don't see Miss Martel."

"Thomas?"

"Her driver."

"Sure, right, of course. I wonder where she could be?"

"Stay here—I'll see what I can find out." Danny thought he'd landed the prize as Jerome disappeared into the club.

"Everything all right, Jerome?" Ruby asked his gatekeeper.

"Maybe. There's a guy outside asking about Miss Martel. Says he was supposed to meet her here—but I think he's bullshit 'cause he didn't know about Thomas."

"Is he wearing a black leather jacket?"

"Yea, he was just inside."

"I'm going to call Vienna now—please wait a moment." Ruby picked up the house phone and called 342-6816. Vienna's phone sat on her dressing room table, but it was also tied into Jordan's bedroom line. He was startled from his sleep when the call came in and quickly gathered himself, assuming her voice.

"Hello, this is Vienna."

"I'm so sorry to bother you this late, darling, but there's someone at the club asking for you." Vienna felt a note of urgency in Ruby's voice.

"Who is it, Ruby?"

"I haven't seen him before—he told Jerome you were supposed to meet tonight, but he didn't know about Thomas. I thought it suspicious."

Vienna thought intently on this. Jordan did as well; this double-think, while not unprecedented, was particularly taxing given the physical exhaustion they both felt.

"Is he still there?" she asked quietly.

"Yes, Vienna—he's waiting for Jerome to give him some information, should you wish to give any whatsoever."

"Have Jerome give him my cross streets, Ruby, but not the address. And tell him I'm away this evening but perhaps will be at the club tomorrow night or Sunday. That will be fine."

"Are you sure, Vienna?" Something about this felt strange to Ruby. Especially after last night.

"Yes, I'm certain, and thank you. I have to go now." Jordan placed the receiver in its cradle and continued sitting on the side of the bed, navigating their thoughts. Perhaps someone would be waiting for Vienna in the daylight. She didn't relish the idea of going back to Ruby's so soon, fielding questions from the likes of Jason and the other gossipy boys. He lay back down, exhausted. Jordan had a 9 a.m. appointment with Detective Ronson, 1 Police Plaza. To view the sketch. To talk about Mr. Saji. He would need his sleep.

Jerome dutifully passed along the limited information that Miss Martel had approved and Danny left the club, believing he'd succeeded in getting what Mika had demanded. On his way to 14th Street, he stopped at the Corner Bistro to call him from a pay phone. Mika said, "Nice job," and hung up. Danny ordered a Stoli and tonic and drank it quickly. Then he ordered another and drank it quickly. *What a fucked up night*, he thought, left a 5 dollar tip and left the bar to catch the trains back to Sheepshead Bay.

Jordan dressed conservatively for his meeting downtown, in suit, tie and double-breasted trench coat. He arrived early—little traffic on a Saturday morning—but was not kept waiting. Detective Ronson himself met Jordan in the lobby and led him to his 4th-floor office. The Major Case Squad did not normally concern itself with homicides, but because of the potential link between Saji's murder and the Kandinsky theft the departments were "cooperating" with each other. The detective led with a few questions about Yusaku Saji. *How long have you known Mr. Saji? What was your relationship exactly? Under what circumstances did you meet? Do you know where his money came from? Have you ever known him to engage in theft, or any transaction that could be considered grand larceny?*

Jordan delivered his answers plainly, no subtext. He'd known Yusaku Saji for approximately 3 years. Had been contacted by him through a mutual acquaintance—Andreas Eklund, Jordan's father. He'd helped Saji negotiate the purchase of two signed Warhol prints, one of Einstein, the other Mao, and a sculpture by David Smith, all documented transactions. He believed he was involved in some sort of finance in Japan. Had never been aware of any illegal activity. Could not fathom a connection between the Kandinsky theft and murder in a night club.

Then Detective Ronson opened his desk drawer and pulled out the sketch. The sketch that Vienna had completed the previous afternoon at the 6th Precinct Station. "Mr. Eklund, please look at this rendering of the murderer as recalled by our one witness." He gave the sketch to Jordan. In spite of the fact that many of the lines and facial shadings had been drawn in her own hand, Jordan nonetheless felt a pang of alarm and discomfort seeing the image. He knew absolutely that this was the killer. But he could not know that—only Vienna could possess that knowledge. He also knew this face in another context. Not the name. The face.

Jordan looked up from the sketch.

"I'm quite certain this man is a security guard at the Guggenheim." Ronson made the connection immediately.

"And the Kandinsky was supposed to be on its way to the Guggenheim," the detective muttered, thinking aloud.

"I might suggest you consider doing two things, detective," Jordan offered. "Show your sketch to Mrs. Kellerman. And bring it to the museum. I believe the connection you're trying to draw between the murder and the theft might become clearer. Assuming this is the murderer." He handed the sketch back to Ronson. "Is there anything else you wanted to ask me?" The detective seemed lost in thought for a moment as if trying to assemble pieces of a puzzle that didn't quite belong together. "Detective? Anything else?" Jordan repeated.

"Um, just one thing, Mr. Eklund. Your connection to all of these individuals—Saji, the Kellerman's, the security guard, your tenant Miss Martel…that's a big coincidence in this line of work, wouldn't you think?"

"The art world is a very small universe, detective. Still, yes, I do find it all a bit disturbing—perhaps especially that my tenant has witnessed a murder…it can't be easy for her. But if these connections lead to the same conclusion, perhaps a fuller picture will be revealed." Ronson widened his eyes.

"A fuller picture?"

"Meaning, I might assume the thief is on someone else's payroll—other than the museum's, of course. And I believe it's possible the buyer for this painting is someone other than Saji. He may simply have been the courier, in behalf of a friend or business associate. There is a market for this sort of thing in Japan, and not all transactions are made through normal channels." Jordan rose from his chair, as did Detective Ronson, extending his hand.

"This has been very helpful, Mr. Eklund, thank you for your time."

"You're welcome, detective. If there's anything else I can be of assistance with, please…"

"That's very kind of you. If Mrs. Kellerman and the Guggenheim confirm what you're saying I'm certain we'll be bringing the suspect in for more than questioning. We'll alert you to any developments."

"Good luck, detective."

Jordan arrived at the Horatio Street entrance to his building just after 10:15. He decided to walk around the corner, to Vienna's side. A car was parked directly across the street from the freight entrance—a blue Ford Galaxy, with two men in the front seat. They were just sitting there, one reading a tabloid the other glancing left to the building. Jordan kept walking, toward the river. Jersey plates. He didn't recognize either man but believed he knew what—who—they were waiting for. But she would never appear. He turned left onto 10th Avenue, then to Horatio again, and up the elevator to his home. The reception for Jean-Michel at Annina's gallery would start at 6 p.m. and end when it ended. By mid-afternoon the men waiting on Gansevoort would be thinking about a Plan B— maybe waiting outside Ruby's. She'd said she would probably be there.

Jordan felt a hollowness inside, a longing for Vienna, as if she had gone far away and could not be reached. Standing in front of the mirror he could barely face himself, unable to summon the logic that might locate a missing person. But this rumination was an indulgence he could little afford at the moment. He was meeting Chiaki Saji for tea in a few hours, to offer his condolences and shock, and perhaps learn something he didn't know about her father. And she—Vienna—would call Thomas and ask him to pick her up at four. Then what? Jordan could think clearly enough to realize he was operating in a state of exhaustion, propelled only by the adrenaline events had sent rushing through his nervous system. Nervous system—he hated believing his actions could be controlled by such a mundane thing. He would need sleep before venturing out again. Was that even possible?

*T*he murmurs, footsteps and shuffling papers seemed amplified in the cavernous courtroom on Centre Street. The gavel, the announcement that Court was "now in session" seemed barely to silence the noise inside Vienna's head. The chamber was stifling with the air of a thousand trials. She felt nauseous, yet determined to maintain her composure.

"The prosecution may call its first witness."

"Your Honor, the People call Vienna Martel to the witness stand."

"Stand here, please. Raise your right hand. Do you promise that the testimony you shall give in the case before this court shall be the truth, the whole truth, and nothing but the truth, so help you God?"

"I do."

"Please state your full name."

"Vienna Juliette Martel."

"You may be seated."

"Miss Martel, please tell the Court where you were on the night of October 28th."

"I believe you're referring to the morning of October 29th?"

"Yes, of course. Approximately 1 a.m. on the morning of October 29. Where were you at that time, Miss Martel?"

"I was seated in a night club in the West Village."

"A place called Ruby's, on Charles Lane?"

"Yes."

"You were called here today because you were a witness to a murder in that club. Is that correct?"

"Yes."

"A man was shot three times in the chest, at point blank

range. Is that correct."

"Yes."

"And the shooter took something from the victim…"

"Yes, a leather bag he'd been holding."

"Is the killer in this courtroom, Miss Martel."

"Yes. That man, sitting over there."

"In your testimony, you stated there were two men involved in the murder."

"Yes."

"But you could only identify one?"

"Both men were wearing masks…but…"

"They were wearing masks? Wouldn't two men wearing masks stand out in a crowd?"

"Mardi Gras masks…party masks—other people were wearing masks too. You've heard of Halloween?"

"Yes, of course. Coming in a few days at that point."

"Yes."

"So the two men were wearing masks, but you were able to identify one of them."

"As he was falling the victim pulled the gunman's mask down, so his face was briefly exposed."

"Miss Martel, we understand the shooting took place at the bar. Were you standing at the bar?"

"I was seated on the other side of the room, as I've said."

"If you were on the other side of the room, and the gunman was facing the victim, how could you see his face?"

"He looked around the room quickly, presumably to see if anyone had seen him."

"And he saw you looking at him…"

"*Objection, Your Honor!*"

"*Overruled. You may answer the question.*"

"*Our eyes met for an instant.*"

"*And what happened next?*"

"*He put the gun in his coat pocket, placed the mask back over his face, said something to his partner and both men left with the leather bag.*"

"*Thank you, Miss Martel. I have no further questions at this time.*"

"*Does the Defense have any questions for this witness.*"

"*We do, Your Honor. Miss Martel, you've stated that you were not standing at the bar but you were seated across the room.*"

"*Yes.*"

"*How far away from the bar do you think you were seated?*"

"*I don't know—perhaps fifteen feet.*"

"*And was the bar area crowded?*"

"*It was fairly crowded, yes.*"

"*And yet nothing impaired your view of these three men?*"

"*People were walking to and from the bar but none preventing me from seeing these men.*"

"*Had you been drinking, Miss Martel.*"

"*Objection!*"

"*Your Honor, Defense would like to establish whether the witness might have been impaired in any other way.*"

"*Continue.*"

"*Miss Martel, had you been drinking that evening?*"

"*I'd had one sip of my Champagne.*"

"*And that's it, one sip.*"

"*Yes. I'd only just arrived at Ruby's ten minutes earlier.*"

"*Had you been drinking, or used any substances such as cocaine or marijuana, prior to going to the club?*"

"*Objection!*"

"*I'll answer the question. The answer is No, I had not.*"

"*So mere moments after entering the club your attention was focused on three men at the bar, which you've said was crowded. Why would that be, Miss Martel?*"

"*The man with the leather bag—he was an older, Japanese gentleman, wearing a business suit. I found it odd seeing such a person in this club. So, yes, you could say my attention was fixed on him, and then the two others.*"

"*How long did you say the face of the gunman was exposed?*"

"*I didn't say.*"

"*Do you think one second? Two seconds?*"

"*Perhaps two.*"

"*And sitting across the room, in a crowded bar, you believe you could identify a man whose face might have been exposed for two seconds? Miss Martel?*"

"*Yes.*"

"*Beyond a doubt?*"

"*I believe so.*"

"*Defense has no further questions at this time, Your Honor.*"

"*You may step down, Miss Martel. Do the People wish to call its next witness in this case?*"

"*We do, Your Honor. The People call Jordan Eklund to the witness stand.*"

"*Jordan Eklund. Is Jordan Eklund in this courtroom?*"

Jordan bolted upright from a theta state of half-sleep, exhausted and perspiring. He would need to shower. He would need to change his suit...

By noon Detective Ronson was showing Vienna's sketch to Mrs. Kellerman in her home, though she'd already sat with a sketch person at the Oyster Bay Cove Police Department the day before, describing the two men who'd removed her Kandinsky. But the image presented to her by Ronson was far more detailed and realistic a portrait than the ones she'd helped create. Still, there was uncertainty in her reaction. "I–I do see a resemblance to one of the men. But he had horn-rimmed glasses and wore a grey woolen flat cap. Weren't you shown the sketch done by the Oyster Bay Cove police, detective?" Detective Ronson admitted he had not seen the other rendering, but said he would make a point of comparing the two. Somewhat embarrassed, he thanked Mrs. Kellerman for her time and left.

An hour later the detective was in the office of Daniel Russo, head of security at the Guggenheim, a tall, thick-boned man who fit the profile of a retired cop. He looked at the sketch, then looked up. "He worked here for about two years, up until last Tuesday—didn't show up for his shift, hasn't shown up since. Mika Pavlou. Is he in trouble?"

"Yes, I'd say so. He's a suspect in the theft of the Kandinsky painting on Thursday, and a murder that took place at a club late Thursday night-Friday morning."

"Jesus Christ. What can I do for you, detective?"

"If you could provide his address, any details on his background, a photo—those things would help a great deal."

"We've got all of that, detective—the museum has a pretty

extensive clearance procedure, especially for security hires. Though maybe we missed somethin' with this guy." Russo stood and walked to a white file cabinet, pulling one of the drawers, then fingering through the folders. "Pavlou…here we go," he said as he plucked out one of the files, handing it to Detective Ronson. "I can make you a copy of any of this." And there it was: a resume covering nearly a lifetime leading to this moment—from grade school near Omonoia Square in Athens to brief service with the Hellenic Police, jumping to porter at the Roosevelt Hotel in Manhattan, waiter, then security guard at Pace Gallery 1977–1980. He'd started at the Guggenheim in late 1980. A phone number and address: 156 Essex Street on the Lower East Side, apartment 3C. Several short letters of recommendation from his former employers. Who wouldn't trust Mr. Pavlou? And a photocopy of his Guggenheim security photo—a near perfect match of the sketch brought by Detective Ronson.

"A copy of these things would be very helpful, Mr. Russo."

"Sure. I'll make them right here, detective." Which he did at the Xerox machine on the shelf behind his desk.

By mid-afternoon the detective had obtained a search warrant for Mika Pavlou's apartment and an arrest warrant for his suspected role in the theft of the Kandinsky, and for the murder of Yusaku Saji. As a courtesy, he would contact Officer Molina from the 6th Precinct and invite him to meet at the apartment. "Yes, of course I'll be there." Molina was a little pissed that these next steps were initiated downtown. *Arrogant pricks.* But that's what "cooperation" was supposed to be about, right? And at least the FBI had been preempted. So, fine.

At 3:45 p.m. Jordan put on his overcoat. He took Vienna's beaded clutch from the lower dresser drawer. It still contained her wallet and a few makeup items. He removed the cash but left her French driver's license and a photo of herself taken during her year at École des Beaux-Arts in Paris. The clutch fit snugly in his coat pocket. He left his home and locked the 8th floor behind him. Outside, the descending sun behind his building cast a shadow over Washington Street. The temperature had already fallen into the low 50's. Tomorrow was Halloween. Then came November. Jordan walked to the corner of Gansevoort. The Galaxy was gone and the block was empty. He walked into the street and stopped directly opposite the service entrance, where he knew Thomas would park in a matter of minutes. He pulled the clutch from his pocket and dropped it close to the center of the road, then walked quickly to the sidewalk and west, looking back to see if anyone had watched. No pedestrians, no commercial traffic. Hopefully, Thomas would recognize the clutch and find Vienna's wallet inside. He would wait a few minutes for her to come out of the building. She was never late. He'd become anxious, cross the street, enter the building and ring her floor. No answer. There was a pay phone in the White Horse Tavern on Hudson and 11th. He would call Ruby's first. *No, we haven't seen Vienna.* His concern merging with fear for her life, he would call the 6th Precinct and report that he had found her purse and wallet in the street in front of her building and that Miss Martel had not kept her appointment to meet him at four and that she did not answer the bell to her floor.

If someone else found the clutch before Thomas, hopefully they would report it to the police—there was nothing of value inside. Well, except for the thing itself, and the Saint Laurent wallet. Hopefully, a good citizen. Then Thomas would wait a bit longer for Vienna, perhaps 15 minutes, before going to the building to ring her floor. He would go back and sit in the car and think about calling Ruby's…maybe even the police…

By 4:15 Jordan had circled the block and was back to the corner of Washington and Horatio. Anxiety and longing filled his body. He felt ill. No one would ever describe him as sentimental, a romantic. But his heart was bursting. Vienna was gone now. Could he actually have taken her life? Soon she would be yet another police report, a 'missing person.' There would be a bulletin and a search. A search of her home. Jordan would be called. Details collided with feelings in his mind. He decided to walk to Chiaki's apartment building on East 17th Street. Breathing would steady with the tempo of his steps. Blood would flow more rapidly from his heart and arteries into his brain. The tide of emotions would ebb, some perspective regained, at least for a while.

But once seated beside Chiaki another wave of emotion flooded Jordan's heart. Her sorrow and shock, more powerful than his fear and emptiness, forced him to absorb someone else's pain. Chiaki's father, Jordan's friend, was dead.

Yusaku Saji had been his first client in New York City, a meeting arranged by Jordan's father in 1979. In part through the successful acquisitions they had consummated together, the art world wunderkind and the Japanese businessman had developed a mutual trust and friendship. If there was an exhibit of particular interest, or a special piece coming on the market, Jordan would make a point of informing Saji. And when his daughter moved to New York City to finish her degree in International Studies Jordan helped her find an apartment in the Gramercy area, not far from the university, and introduced her to many of his young colleagues.

"I'm so sorry, Chiaki—there are no words." No words, and no way to console someone in the face of a fatal loss.

"Thank you for coming, Jordan," she said, trying to steady her voice. "It's impossible to understand. My father had no enemies, only people who respected him. Who would do this?"

"There had to have been people involved whom he didn't know, a scheme he was unaware of. I don't know if you could have heard, but the police are linking your father's killers with the theft of a valuable painting the morning before."

"He would never steal from anyone!"

"Of course not, Chiaki, but perhaps someone in whose behalf he was acting made Mr. Saji an unknowing participant. They've identified the man with the gun—when he is found more will be known. But nothing that could incriminate your father, I'm certain of that."

"I am in mourning, yet I am angry and frustrated to be powerless and without answers. And there's nothing I can do for my father now." Tears welled up in Chiaki's unblinking eyes. Jordan searched the place where there were no words.

"Even when the answers come and the murderers are caught, it won't be nearly enough. But I will do what I can, to assist the police, and to help you, Chiaki. Are arrangements being made now for your father?"

"I will take father to Tokyo on Monday—the earliest they would allow. My uncle is taking care of the arrangements. He will meet me at the airport...the funeral will be Thursday... and father will be buried with my mother in Yanaka Cemetery."

"I could accompany you, Chiaki. This is a terrible burden for a daughter to bear alone."

"That's very kind of you, Jordan—but I'm just going through the motions now. The details are taken care of; I'll be there for the documentation, his and mine. I'll sleep on the flight, visit and mourn with my relatives, struggle with their questions. Then return the following week to resume school. But thank you."

Jordan shared what he knew of the Kandinsky theft, and of the suspect who had worked at the Guggenheim. Then he left the topic and asked Chiaki about her school year, but there were difficult silences as they sipped their cups of sencha tea. No words. Finally he rose.

"I am here if you need anything, Chiaki—please know that."

"I do, and I'm grateful, Jordan." They held each other for a long moment before Jordan left the apartment and resumed walking.

It was after 7 and dark when he arrived at Annina's gallery on Prince Street. Inside, animated chatter filled the room, along with clinking glasses and smoke from cigarettes and weed. Jean-Michel's paintings took up all of two walls, his drawings covered a third. Gitanes in one hand, Chablis in the other, the artist held court for friends and hangers-on. Abrielle, never the clinging girlfriend, flitted about the room, making "connections." Warhol, out of deference to his friend, stood in a far corner, surrounded by a few of his ersatz "superstars." Annina herself mingled from friend to patron, never letting the party distract from business. Then she sighted Jordan and quickly excused herself to meet him at the door. "So happy you made it, Jordan—I was starting to worry! The gallery's been packed practically since I opened the door!"

Jordan summoned all of himself to the moment. "I would *never* have missed a chance to celebrate Jean-Michel, Annina."

"Of course you wouldn't! Now let me take your coat and let's get you a glass of something—I think it's going to be a long night." Annina pulled Jordan's coat from his shoulders, took his hand and ushered him through the crowd toward a counter where the bar had been set up. She turned to her bartender with instructions, "Adrian, please pour our friend a drink while I hang up his coat." But Jordan's emotions had not waited outside the gallery.

"Annina, I need to use your phone for a moment, then we'll celebrate, I promise."

"Oh for Christ' sake. Follow me." She led him to her office and pointed to the desk. "You have five minutes before I come back for you!"

Annina closed the door behind her and Jordan picked up the phone. First directory assistance, then 1 Police Plaza. The number rang 12 times before a disinterested female voice came on the line.

"NYPD can I help you."

"Detective Ronson, please."

"Detective Ronson is tied up—who's calling?"

"Please tell him Jordan Eklund is on the line."

"Hold please." Instead of being put on "hold" she'd just laid the phone on her desk. Jordan listened to the sounds of a busy police station on a Saturday night. Voices, phones, intercom. Several minutes passed before the detective picked up.

"This is Ronson."

"This is Jordan Eklund, detective. I hope it's not inappropriate to have called."

"Not at all, Mr. Eklund. In fact, I tried to reach you earlier… but go ahead."

"I'm at a gallery event on Prince Street and all anyone can speak of is the Kandinsky theft. It's not my intention to comment on this matter publicly, detective, but I do wonder if there were any developments since we met."

"Yes, a few. The man you'd identified from the sketch did in fact work at the Guggenheim, though he hasn't shown up there since last week. His name is Mika Pavlou. Unfortunately, Mrs. Kellerman was unable to make a positive ID from our sketch—it seems he was wearing a cap and glasses at the time of the robbery."

"That is unfortunate."

"Well the sketch she helped render with the Oyster Bay

Cove police showed enough resemblance that we were able to get search and arrest warrants for both crimes."

"So that sounds like good news, detective."

"*Not quite* good news, I'm afraid. The apartment was empty—no Pavlou, no weapons, cash, anything we could call evidence. It's unclear whether he knows he's being sought, but he's definitely not taking chances. Of course we have his building under surveillance. But the reason for my earlier call, Mr. Eklund, is that a half hour ago I heard from Officer Molina at the 6th Precinct. It seems Vienna Martel is missing." Jordan paused, as the action he had plotted played out in real time, with the ending unknown.

"Miss Martel is *missing?* How could that be, detective?"

"Her driver found her purse and wallet in the street, in front of her building. She was supposed to meet him there three hours ago, but she never showed up."

"This is very disturbing…do you think she's in danger? Have you begun a search?" At that moment Annina opened the door and was about to lunge for the phone when Jordan raised his hand, waving her off impatiently.

"Of course we have. But little is known about her. She hangs out sometimes at a place called Ruby's. The driver takes her on errands, shopping, visiting friends at night…"

"And she's the murder witness."

"Indeed, Mr. Eklund. And if she doesn't appear by morning we'll need to search her residence. You have the key I presume."

"Yes, of course."

"Please be available in the morning. And thank you again for your assistance in identifying the suspect. Very helpful."

"You're welcome, detective. Hopefully Miss Martel is safe and will return to her home."

"We hope so, too. Have a good night, Mr. Eklund." Jordan placed the phone on its receiver then was motionless. All these hidden pieces, now in plain sight. Except that Vienna was missing. The emptiness was returning. He shook his head sharply, turned away from the desk then stopped, searching for another piece. He could feel her inside. She was watching him, wondering, *What will you do now?* What made him believe she would simply die in the street, inside a beaded clutch? How presumptuous. Cowardly. Vienna could not be dead, because the man who killed Yusaku Saji was still alive. Jordan left Annina's office. The gallery was loud and festive. Annina, now beside Jean-Michel, had been watching her door and spotted Jordan immediately, waving him to come. And he did, smiling broadly.

"It's about time, darling—no more phone calls tonight!"

"Where have you been for fuck's sake?!" the artist chided as he took his friend's hand and pulled him closer for a hug.

"I'm fully present, my friend, you have my word. It's been a long day, with this Kandinsky thing, and the murder—I was just on the phone with the detective downtown, but that's enough for tonight. This seems to be a brilliant opening…you both must be thrilled."

"Yea, it's really cool—look at all these crazies!" Jean-Michel smiled sarcastically. "But truth is, man, I'm really looking forward to Edinburgh—I've never been." Annina pretended to take offense.

"Oh, and this is *nothing*," she sneered.

"Of course it's not *nothing*, Annina—you're half the reason for the show in Scotland, darling!"

"You two souls are perfect for each other," Jordan mediated. "I may actually come see you for the Fruitmarket show, Jean-Michel."

"You'd fly to Edinburgh just for the show, Jordan?" the artist asked incredulously.

"I thought of going to Paris first, and trying to connect with a friend there…so perhaps after."

"New York, Paris, Edinburgh—you're too much, Jordan. I'll go fetch you that drink you never got…what will it be?"

"Something with bubbles, Annina. Then we'll have a toast."

Guests—invited and not—were still arriving at Annina's gallery when Jordan excused himself just before 9:30, in spite of protests from gallerist and artist alike. "I have a 10:00 p.m. call to Tokyo—where it will be 11 a.m. tomorrow—which I'm *definitely* not making from your office, Annina. But I will see you both sooner than later."

The 10:00 p.m. call would actually be to Thomas. Mika Pavlou had not been arrested. Therefore he needed to believe that the witness to the murder was still alive, still needing to be "handled." And Jordan needed to know that Yusaku Saji was not an accomplice in the events that led to his murder. And to acknowledge a raw pulse beating inside him—Vienna's plea for her freedom.

"Hello, Thomas."

"Miss Martel?"

"I'm sorry I couldn't keep our appointment this afternoon..."

"I–I was worried. When I found your purse and wallet in the street I thought something terrible might have happened—so I called the police."

"You did the right thing, Thomas. I was frightened, too. I saw two men waiting in a car outside my building this morning—I believe they're somehow involved with the murder. I believe they were waiting for me."

"Jesus Christ! I mean, how did your purse get there? Did they attack you?"

"I put it there, after they'd left, and just before you were to arrive. I wanted to disappear, not be involved in this ugly business any further...to be 'missing.' And that's what happened. But these men—whoever they are—are free. Which means I cannot be."

"So what will you do, Miss Martel? What can *I* do?"

"There's nothing to do at this moment, Thomas. But I'd like you to take me back to Ruby's tomorrow night."

"But the police think you're missing!"

"I'll call them in the morning and tell them what I've just told you. Do you have my purse and wallet?"

"Yes, ma'am."

"Then perhaps you could bring it tomorrow night. Can you pick me up at 10:45, Thomas?"

"Sure, of course. But..."

"Yes?"

"Tomorrow is..."

"Halloween."

"It will be crowded—it could be dangerous…"

"I suppose. But I'll protect you, Thomas." Vienna couldn't resist the tease. "Now have a good night, and thank you."

"No, I'll protect you, Miss Martel. And *you* have a good night."

When Jordan first provided Thomas with an introduction to Vienna, he didn't fully imagine the importance this driver might have in her life. Of course he'd considered her safety and comfort during downtown late night excursions— that was the idea. But he hadn't anticipated their unforced closeness, nor what a relationship with her sole heterosexual companion might mean. Had Thomas become as much the older, protective brother as the responsible employee? Right now the employee was focused on the unfolding events, trying to understand what was happening, but he could not. He knew nothing of the Kandinsky theft, nor of Mr. Saji's relationship to Jordan. Only that there was a murder and Miss Martel was the witness and now her life was in danger. At least she was alive.

Jordan hung up Vienna's phone and stared in the direction of her home, on the other side of his bedroom wall. His anxiety had ebbed, a calm come over him. He felt her there, which was reassuring. Still, it was too early to sleep, no matter how much his body required it. He brushed his hair, straightened his tie and took the elevator to the lobby. It was less than a fifteen-minute walk to Ruby's, where it was unlikely anyone would know him. He would simply walk by on the other side of Charles Lane as if to another destination. Just look to see if the club was busy on a Saturday night. See if the Galaxy was nearby. Forty people or so waited along a velvet rope to enter Ruby's, many in masks. Busy night. A blue Galaxy parked a hundred feet away, close to Washington Street. No one inside.

Having resolved what their course of action would be over the next 24 hours, Jordan collapsed into a deep sleep. Yet it would be Vienna's dreams he would awaken from. A dream of Paris. Her beloved Hotel Caron de Beaumarchais, with its ancient furnishings and artwork, where she'd lived for nearly a month at the start of a school year. Lost in reverie at the Jeu de Paume. Ending the day at Les Deux Magots. The short walk to Quai Voltaire…being followed, by an admirer? She never found out. They must return to Paris, he thought, as soon as things were finished here. Hopefully, very soon.

Jordan made a light breakfast for himself. Coffee, toast with blackberry jam, slices of orange. Then Vienna called the 6th Precinct station and asked for Officer Molina. "He's not on duty today, can someone else help you?"

"This is Vienna Martel—yesterday someone called your station and reported that I was missing. I'm calling to report that I'm not."

"Please hold, ma'am." She waited a full minute, listening to the babel and din in the station. Then an Asian woman's voice came on the line.

"Miss Martel, this is Officer Huang. I accompanied you to the station with Officer Molina the night of the murder."

"Yes, I remember you."

"And we did hear, from your driver I believe, that you were missing—that he'd found your purse and wallet in the street." Vienna shared the details of her scheme with Officer Huang. Her fear of being hunted by the murderers, the men waiting outside her building. Her plan to be "missing," to arrange for her own disappearance.

"It seemed you'd succeeded, but you're calling us now…"

"This morning I realized that until these men are caught I will remain in danger."

"If they are in fact looking for you, that is correct, Miss Martel."

"I did not leave my home Friday night, officer, but I was told that a man was asking for me at Ruby's. I'm planning to go back there tonight, which is the reason I've called you."

"I would caution you against doing that, ma'am. Halloween is a crazy night downtown, especially in the Village. If someone is looking for you there will be enough noise and confusion to cover their actions—as there was three nights ago."

"I'm well aware of that, officer. But the club's owner and staff know me well and will look after me. If the police decide to come I would suggest after eleven, and not in uniform, nor in official cars. If you see a blue Galaxy on the street, you will know they are there."

"Miss Martel, we can't guarantee your safety if you do this. I strongly urge you…"

"Thank you for your concern, Officer Huang. I will be careful." Vienna hung up the phone leaving Huang without another rebuttal. Frustrated, she thought for a moment, then reluctantly decided to call Officer Molina at his home on Staten Island—after all, this was pretty much his case. Molina was not happy. The family was getting ready for church. Not that he was a believer, but his wife liked the ritual for the kids. No point in arguing with that. It was Sunday. Halloween. Later he would take the kids trick or treating—the streets in New

Brighton were safe enough. But that would be early. *Shit, it's fucking Sunday.* He decided to call Detective Ronson. After all, the departments were "cooperating." Ronson was actually excited by this development—he had no other plans for Halloween.

Next Vienna called Ruby's and left a message on the machine— she would be coming to the club tonight, looked forward to seeing everyone. This way if anyone asked for her, the answer might be 'She's expected.' Then a call to Thomas, asking that he bring a mask for himself when he came to pick her up so that he might accompany her into Ruby's. He understood that to mean *Be my bodyguard for the night.* He was honored to be asked, but what kind of mask? Vienna would wear her silver Venetian Swan mask.

Twelve hours until Thomas would come for Vienna. Normally so organized, so in control of details and outcomes, Jordan was restive, with no plan for filling the time. He realized he hadn't spoken with his father since before the murder of his friend. Is it possible he hadn't heard? Neither crime would have been in the papers yet and Andreas Eklund never watched—did not possess—a television. Only listened to classical music on the radio. It would be late afternoon in Salzburg. The call would be nearly as difficult as his meeting with Chiaki. They spoke in Austro-Bavarian, Mr. Eklund's native dialect. Devastated by the news of his friend Yusaku, Jordan waited as his father stammered for words and his breathing settled. "I'm sorry, father, I'm so sorry to bring you this news." Jordan asked if he had spoken with Mr. Saji recently. His father hesitated.

"Yes. I spoke with Yusaku in September. I asked if I might put another Japanese business man in contact with him..."

The other Japanese businessman, Tomiichi Nakano, had been seeking a trusted individual who could assist in expediting a large financial transaction in the United States. The purchase of a painting. Mr. Saji had been happy to accommodate his friend. Father and son did not speak of the obvious connection. Jordan urged Mr. Eklund not to attempt to contact Mr. Nakano. There was no purpose until more was known of both crimes and those who had plotted them. He told his father of his meeting with Chiaki and the plans for Mr. Saji's funeral in Tokyo. Mr. Eklund wondered aloud, as Jordan had, whether he should attend. His son told him it would not be the right time, but he would keep him informed of developments. "Much more will be known very soon, I'm certain of that, father."

Jordan walked to one of the south-facing windows in his loft. Hands clasped behind his back, he stared at the distant harbor, and the boats. He couldn't possibly spend the rest of the day and half the night pacing the floor, so he decided to walk around the Village. Kids would already be trick-or-treating. The bridge and tunnel revelers would be arriving early to the Irish pubs. Barricades and police would have taken their positions on 10th Street in preparation for the parade. Plenty of distractions before indulging in a long brunch at La Ripaille.

It was nearly 5 when he left the bistro, the taste of jambon et fromage crepe and three café noisettes still in his mouth. The cool air was bracing, the sidewalks alive with costumed partiers and the merely curious. Jordan kept moving, east from Hudson Street, then south on Bleecker. Bars, clubs, second-hand clothing shops, head shops, the now fading markers of the folkie and new wave eras. A mix of fallen leaves and trash blown to the curb. Then something caught his eye in a parlor floor shop window. Along with the hookahs and beads, costumed mannequins. Standing next to Richard Nixon and Darth Vader was David Bowie, as "Aladdin Sane," one of his many alter egos. Jordan had met Bowie a few years earlier, at a gallery in London. In their eyes, he'd sensed recognition of a kindred identity, their androgynous beauty. Though formally courteous and deferential, inside Jordan had suppressed a profound attraction. Or was he simply star stricken by the beautiful rock idol?

What if he—she—Vienna—were to arrive at Ruby's *as Bowie*…as Aladdin Sane? Physically, they could easily have been brothers, or sisters. And how difficult could it be to mimic Bowie's South London accent? To most Americans, his Volksschule-learned English sounded perfectly British. Jordan walked up the stoop and into the store. She wouldn't need the Aladdin mask. Just some glitter and face paint. The two-tone lightning bolt across her forehead and right cheek would take time. But there was time. Vienna had extravagant leotards a friend had brought from Milan she'd sworn she'd never wear. And maroon knee boots. Jordan could color his hair orange-blonde and tease it to a fluffy crown, like Bowie's. He could shave his eyebrows—well, they'd have to think about that.

By eight-thirty Jordan had dyed, blown and sprayed his hair. He thought it looked quite silly, so very *not* Jordan—or Vienna—yet he felt a mix of excitement and trepidation. Was this really a disguise? Would her face not be fully visible? Well of course it would, yet completely unexpected, and that was the point, wasn't it? They would finish dressing in Vienna's suite, where the facial lighting and mirrors were more practical. Now, wearing only his briefs, Jordan walked from his bath to the bedroom. From the lowest drawer of his desk, he removed a Beretta M1935, a gift from his father, who'd served in the Austrian Resistance during Nazi occupation. He checked the magazine. It contained eight rounds. He then went to his dresser and removed Vienna's breasts and brassiere. With this incongruous collection in both hands, he left his loft and entered Vienna's home. She was no longer a missing person.

It took over an hour and a half to complete her 'mask.' White eyeliner applied to the brows (no shaving—they couldn't imagine how Jordan might explain that to…whomever); a pale magenta gloss on the eyelids and lips; a thin, black tracing along the hairline, to suggest the possibility of a wig? It seemed plausible. And, most time consuming, creating the two-toned bolt across the face. Fortunately, Vienna was quite proficient at figure rendering. When finally finished she considered herself in the mirror, and in fact found him quite attractive. It even seemed somehow wrong to apply her breasts, as if she would be violating him. *It's a costume, Vienna…please remember that.* She had to search another dresser for the boldly striped, Italian leotards. Skin-tight and shiny, she began to feel aroused. A fitted yellow-metallic off-shoulder top (which she would *never* wear) and vintage flamenco vest nearly completed the look and distracted from her small breasts as well. Now the knee boots. *Awful.* And, eyes closed, a pinch of glitter on the face. *Jesus Christ, who am I?*

Hanging from the armoire door, a saffron-dyed, ostrich messenger bag—it seemed a fitting accessory for Bowie—inside she placed the Beretta, and on top of the gun, a carefully folded silk scarf. She stood for a final appraisal of her new persona, singing softly with a faint smile, *Turn and face the strange...Ch-ch-changes.*

It was almost eleven when Vienna stepped out of her building and onto Gansevoort. Thomas, waiting outside the Mercedes, ignored her as she approached. It couldn't be her.

"Hello, Thomas. Thank you for waiting," she greeted, channeling the voice of the famous Londoner.

"Miss Martel? Is that...you?" Thomas slapped his forehead in disbelief.

"It *was* me, Thomas. But now it's David Bowie. What do you think?"

"Um. I...can hardly believe what I'm seeing!"

"Well it's Halloween, after all. And nothing is quite what it seems, is it?"

"No, ma'am, it certainly isn't." Thomas moved to open the passenger door but Vienna interrupted.

"You go ahead, Thomas, I'm going to walk to Ruby's."

"But it's cold outside, ma'am."

"It's a short walk. If someone sees the car they'll assume I'm inside. But when Mr. Bowie arrives no one will have a clue. Do you understand, Thomas?"

"I think so, Miss Martel."

"So wait before you come in. I'll let Jerome know. Did you bring a mask?"

"Yes, ma'am." He reached into the front window and pulled out a Ronald Reagan mask.

"Good Lord," she mocked, shaking her head. "Okay, I'll see you at Ruby's. And don't park too close. Oh, and my purse, Thomas?"

"Yes, right here."

"Leave it for now." With that, Vienna turned and walked south on Washington and Thomas got in the car. By now the streets and sidewalks were crowded and noisy with costumed life. The parade was over and thousands of freakish marchers and onlookers had dispersed to bars, parties, stoops and empty lots with open bottles and joints. The cops couldn't be bothered unless there was a real problem. A stabbing, whatever. Vienna was recipient of a few catcalls and sideways glances as she walked. The gay boys *loved* Aladdin Sane. She smiled and waved and kept walking.

On Charles Lane, she could see the big Mercedes parked down the block from the club, close to West Street. She approached the car and nodded to Thomas, holding up a hand to say "Not just yet." In front of Ruby's there were dozens of people milling about, half of them in line to get in, the others smoking, plotting, hooking up. Some in costumes, some with painted faces, all with temporary identities. Sunday night in the Village. Vienna paused and surveyed the scene. Then another vehicle appeared, pulling up directly behind Thomas. A blue Galaxy. There were three men inside. Her heart began to race. *Will the police come?* she wondered. But no one could possibly know who she was. She walked decisively along the velvet rope to the head of the line.

"Sir, there is a line and you'll have to wait, like everyone else," Jerome instructed with impassive authority.

"Jerome, it's Vienna."

"Miss Martel?" he responded, genuinely confused.

"Yes…I've come in disguise you might say."

"We heard you might come, but I never never would have…"

"Well it's good to be here again. I've missed everyone!"

"Go right inside, and tell Ruby it's you."

As Jerome held the door for Vienna she breezily instructed, "Oh, and I've asked Thomas to join me as well, and if any of my friends ask for me please tell them to look for David Bowie."

"Of course, Mr. Bowie. Happy Halloween!"

Inside, the house was already filled—the lounge seating, the bar, the standing room in between. The music and raised voices were a cacophonous mix as "Sympathy For The Devil" howled from the dance floor. This was one night the fire marshals would pass on. Vienna snaked her way forward and found Ruby at his usual station, helplessly 'chaperoning' his party. She moved in close, inches from his ear. "Ruby, it's

Vienna." Startled, he turned and believed he was staring at David Bowie. "It's me, Vienna," she repeated.

"My God! I would *never* have known that, Vienna!" He kissed her on both cheeks and pulled her close. "It is so good to know that you're all right, that you're here tonight!"

"I couldn't be anywhere else, my friend—it's Halloween, after all."

"Let's get you Champagne…then we'll make room on your banquette…." But Vienna waved a finger in protest.

"Not just yet, Ruby. Believe it or not, I'm going to the dance floor—I'm quite certain it's what my alter ego would do. If any one asks for me, please tell them to look for Mr. Bowie…and I'll see you in a bit."

"Absolutely, darling." With that, she touched Ruby's cheek and inched toward the dance floor, where the crowd bent to the will of the DJ.

Billy Idol, "Dancing With Myself." Perfect. And that's what Vienna did, in the center of the floor, with the modestly seductive moves of an androgynous rock star. Boys and girls alike moved in to share a dance with this alluring beauty, and she accommodated them all, in their turn, with a faint smile.

Inside the blue Galaxy, the man in the back seat spoke. "If that's her car and driver, then she's inside, and I'll recognize her."

"Want me to come too?" Danny asked, hoping the answer was No.

"No, wait here for me. This can't get fucking messed up." Pavlou put on a mask—this time a generic clown face—and left the car. Thomas had noticed. He quickly removed his jacket and shirt, revealing a black tank top and the tattoo of a snake running from his left wrist to his bicep, roughly parallel with a three-inch scar on his forearm—vestiges of an earlier time in the Seton Hill neighborhood of Baltimore. He put on the Reagan mask and left the car quickly. Dimitri and Danny, transfixed by the uninhibited street life all around them, weren't focusing on the man in a wife beater. Jockeying to the front of the line, Pavlou was face-to-face with Jerome, who wasn't having it.

"You'll have to wait in line, buddy, like everyone else."

"Vienna asked me to meet her here…do you know if she's arrived?"

Jerome stamped the back of the clown's hand. "Look for David Bowie," he replied impatiently, waving him past. Moments later, Thomas was standing at the front of the line, but before Jerome could send him to the rear, he lifted his mask.

"Jerome, it's Thomas, Miss Martel's driver. She asked me to come inside tonight," he spoke with urgency in his voice.

"Yes, she said to expect you. Look for David Bowie." Thomas put his Reagan face back on and entered the fray.

Vienna moved fluidly to the rhythm of each song, from "Tainted Love" to "Sexual Healing," which the DJ had brought back from Belgium months before its release in the States. Her eyes were half shut, as if in an induced trance. At the art auctions, at the negotiating table, you never revealed your emotions. Remained impassive. But always alert. She noticed someone standing on the perimeter of the dance floor, not moving. Wearing a clown mask, a long coat, not moving. She ignored his gaze and kept turning slowly to the sensuous beat, the dancers pulsating around her. Then she spotted the Reagan mask near the back of the room. She nodded, acknowledging Thomas' presence. When the song transitioned to the opening bassline of "Under Pressure," she stopped dancing, bowing appreciatively to her admirers. And, walking past Thomas, she said without looking at him, "If a clown follows me, wait one minute before coming down." She continued, unhurriedly, to the basement steps, illuminated by candle sconces, which led to the two WC's. Vienna entered the one whose door was cracked open. There was a toilet with no stall, a urinal, a sink, more candle lighting. She left the door unlocked and faced the mirror above the sink. How beautiful she was in the low lighting. She placed her open bag in the basin and with her right hand gripped the Beretta firmly. The door opened and was quickly shut and locked by a man in a clown mask, whom she now saw in the mirror.

"I know who you are," he said. She turned to face him as he was pulling something from his coat pocket.

"I don't believe you do, sir," Vienna replied and fired into his forearm. He recoiled in pain, pulling his empty hand from the pocket, gripping his arm with the other. "But I'm quite sure I know who you are."

"Fucking bitch!" Pavlou shouted, angrily rushing Vienna before she could fire again. He pinned her against the brick wall by the sink, his upper body pushing the wounded forearm against her throat, his left hand gripping her wrist. "You saw something you shouldn't have the other night, lady." He couldn't have anticipated the sinewy strength of Vienna and Jordan's limbs. Her right knee jerked sharply into his groin, sending a bolt of pain up his spine. "Aggh...fucking...you are dead!" he screamed, pushing harder against her throat and effectively neutralizing the Beretta. Vienna was unable to speak or cry out as she gasped for breath.

On the other side of the door, Thomas knocked loudly, calling her name, shaking the handle. He backed up two feet and threw his entire weight, shoulder first, into the door. It flew open. Seeing Vienna pinned against the wall, he gripped his hands together over his head and brought them down decisively into the back of Pavlou's neck causing him to buckle to his knees. Thomas bent down, placed his neck in a stranglehold, pulled the injured arm behind his back and stood him upright. Vienna pulled the gun from Pavlou's coat pocket and lifted the mask from his head.

"This is the one I saw murder the Japanese man. And this is the gun." Thomas saw that Vienna had a gun in each hand.

"But you could have killed him!"

"He'd have very little to say if he were dead, wouldn't you agree, Thomas?" She put the mask back over Pavlou's head. "We'll walk him to the front of the house—there's no reason to make a scene, he'll just be another drunken clown at a Halloween party." She then addressed the murderer. "If you try anything, Thomas will break your arm and your neck simultaneously—and I *will* shoot you. I hope that's understood." Under the circumstances, he could neither speak nor nod, but offered no resistance. Vienna put both weapons in her bag and they left the john, which two men in matching costumes immediately entered. Another bathroom break.

It was a challenge getting through the crowded dance floor and more so the narrow bar, but Bowie blithely led the way. At the front of the bar, she could see Ruby talking with a man in a grey suit. It was Detective Ronson, whom Vienna had never met and whom she now ignored.

"Ruby, may I speak with you?" she interrupted, with Thomas and their captive standing behind her.

"Vienna! This man is looking for you. He says he's with the police downtown. I hope there's no trouble tonight!" Ronson stared at the strange creature speaking with Ruby. She seemed familiar…because she so closely resembled the figure she had costumed to be? Perhaps.

"Miss Martel?" he probed.

"Yes, and you are?"

"Detective Ronson, from the Major Crime Unit downtown. You were the witness to a murder here last Thursday, is that correct?"

"Friday morning, to be precise. And this is the murderer." Vienna turned and pulled the mask over Mika's head. "Does he look familiar to you, detective?"

"Yes, but how…" Vienna cut him off, opening her bag and pulling out the long-barreled weapon.

"And this is the gun he used to kill that man, and intended to use to kill me tonight." She handed over the weapon but kept her own concealed. "I'm sorry, I should have introduced my dear friend Thomas, who helped me greatly this evening." Ronson, attempting to take control, pulled handcuffs from his suit pocket.

"We'll take it from here, Miss Martel," he assured her, fastening the steel ring to the prisoner's free hand as Thomas released the other. Mika winced in pain. The detective noticed the wound. "What happened to his arm?"

"I had to defend myself, detective." Vienna quickly changed the subject. "And there may be others waiting for him outside."

"There are four officers on the street, holding two men who were sitting in a blue Ford Galaxy. They'll all be going to the 6th Precinct tonight. I'm sure we'll be in touch with you, ma'am."

"I've given my statement, sat with your sketch person and now delivered your murderer, detective," Vienna replied dismissively. "I'm sure these men will have stories to tell but, as you suggested, perhaps you can 'take it from here.'" Ronson left Ruby's, leading Mika Pavlou by his elbow. Vienna followed to see what she had hoped—two unmarked sedans down the street from the blue Galaxy, a man sitting in the back seat of each, a plain-clothed cop at the wheel, two plain-clothed cops waiting, backs against the cars. Officer Molina and Officer Huang. As she walked back into the club she saw the puzzled look on the gatekeeper's face. "Everything's fine, Jerome—there's always a bit of craziness on Halloween, isn't there?"

"Yes, indeed, Miss Vienna."

Vienna knew Detective Ronson would call Jordan in the morning. Mrs. Kellerman would positively identify the men who'd taken the Kandinsky painting from her home. There would be negotiations for further information. Time served for names and places.

"Is everything all right, Vienna?"

"Yes, Ruby, it's fine. And it's Halloween, perhaps we should celebrate."

"Something with bubbles?"

"You know me well. And you, Thomas?"

On Wednesday, November 3rd, Jordan flew to Paris, where he and Vienna would spend eight nights—it would be a much-needed respite from the tragedy and uncertainties of the previous days. And a chance for each to reconnect with their respective friends and colleagues in La Ville Lumière. Then, on the 12th, he would fly to Edinburgh for the opening of Jean-Michel's show at Fruitmarket Gallery. He'd said he might, but it would still be a great surprise for the artist-provocateur. On his answering machine Jordan left word of his travel dates, that he would be staying in Paris in the apartment of a friend, would be checking daily for messages, looked forward to returning to New York City on the 16th. But left no overseas contact information.

On Tuesday, November 2nd, Vienna recorded a message on her answering machine informing any who might call that she would be traveling Upstate for the next few weeks, would unfortunately not be able to check her messages but looked forward to returning after Thanksgiving. "…Please enjoy your holiday and I'll see you after." She then phoned Thomas to tell him she was going away till late November, to stay with a friend on Lake George and take a much-needed break from the city. No, she wouldn't need a ride—she'd take the bus or train and just do some reading. And he would have time to focus on his studies. "But I expect to be back on the 28th. And what will you do for Thanksgiving, Thomas?"

Thomas felt a pang of sadness at the thought that Miss Martel would be away for so long, a feeling he hadn't experienced before. "Um, I won't have any classes that week…I guess my sister and I will drive to Baltimore early and spend it with my mom and some of the other relatives. I hadn't thought about it, though." There was an awkward pause as Vienna lingered over an emotion she hadn't felt, or acknowledged before. The way that a part of Thomas might somehow be inside of her now. The possibility that she could miss him, even for a brief few weeks. What was this?

"Well, hmm. Why don't we have an early Thanksgiving together, Thomas, just you and I? Do you have plans this evening?"

"I…no, I don't." Stumbling for words, stumbling for thoughts. Something was moving inside of him, yet beyond his imagination.

"Could you pick me up at seven then—I'd love to show you a wonderful little bistro in the Village, my treat. Would that be all right?"

"Yes, um, that would be fine, Miss Martel—but please, uh, we have to go Dutch."

"As you wish. And tonight you'll have to call me 'Vienna,' Thomas."

"Yes, Miss Vienna."

"Just 'Vienna.'"

ABOUT THE AUTHOR

Lyle Greenfield is a writer of stories and letters. In his early career he was an advertising copywriter and creative director. In 1980 he planted a vineyard and built a winery in Bridgehampton, Long Island. In 1989 he opened Bang Music in New York City and was a founding member and past president of the Association of Music Producers (AMP). He resides with his wife, Mary Jane Hantz Greenfield, in Amagansett and New York City.